for our mothers

Ellen Beck
Sybil Wilson

and Ellen Watts

Contents

Pudding and Pie

Chosen by Sarah Williams   Illustrated by Ian Beck

OXFORD

UNIVERSITY PRESS

Great Clarendon Street, Oxford OX2 6DP

Oxford University Press is a department of the University of Oxford.
It furthers the University's objective of excellence in research,
scholarship, and education by publishing worldwide in

Oxford New York

Auckland Cape Town Dar es Salaam Hong Kong Karachi
Kuala Lumpur Madrid Melbourne Mexico City Nairobi
New Delhi Shanghai Taipei Toronto

With offices in

Argentina Austria Brazil Chile Czech Republic France Greece
Guatemala Hungary Italy Japan Poland Portugal Singapore
South Korea Switzerland Thailand Turkey Ukraine Vietnam

Oxford is a registered trade mark of Oxford University Press
in the UK and in certain other countries

First published 1989
This paperback edition 2006

British Library Cataloguing in Publication Data

Data available

ISBN-13: 978-0-19276323-5
ISBN-10: 0-19-276323-7
ISBN-13 (book and CD edition): 978-0-19-275477-6
ISBN-10 (book and CD edition): 0-19-275477-7

1 3 5 7 9 10 8 6 4 2

Printed in China by Imago

Boys and girls come out to play

Boys and girls come out to play,
The moon doth shine as bright as day.
Leave your supper and leave your sleep,
And join your playfellows in the street.

6

Come with a whoop and come with a call,
Come with a good will or not at all.
Up the ladder and down the wall,
A half-penny loaf will serve us all;
You find milk and I'll find flour,
And we'll have a pudding in half an hour.

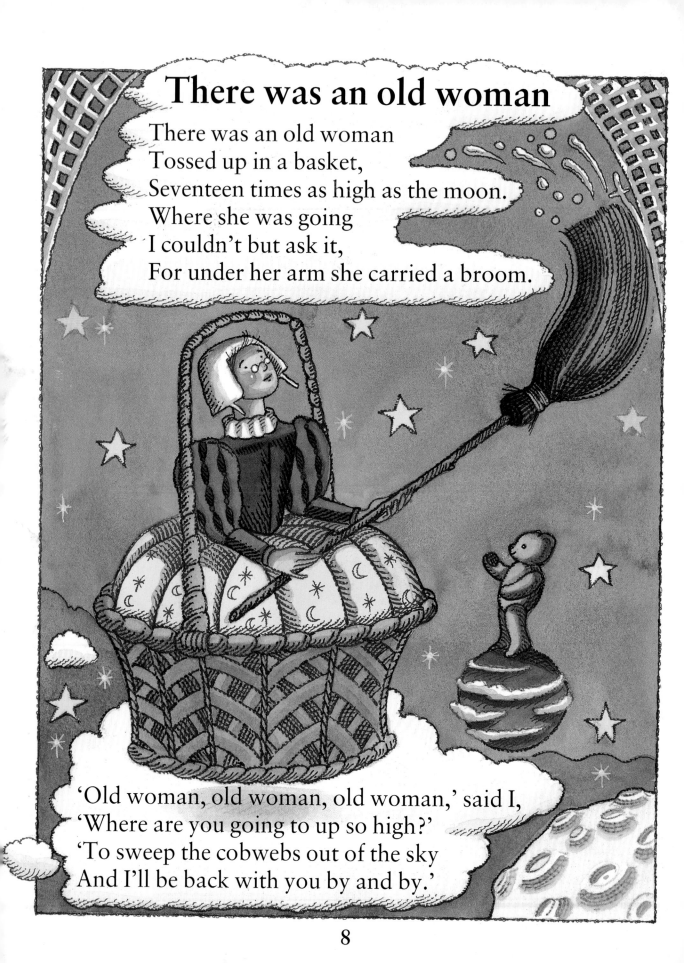

There was an old woman

There was an old woman
Tossed up in a basket,
Seventeen times as high as the moon.
Where she was going
I couldn't but ask it,
For under her arm she carried a broom.

'Old woman, old woman, old woman,' said I,
'Where are you going to up so high?'
'To sweep the cobwebs out of the sky
And I'll be back with you by and by.'

Little Miss Muffet

Little Miss Muffet
Sat on a tuffet,
Eating her curds and whey.
Along came a spider,
Who sat down beside her
And frightened Miss Muffet away.

Pudding and pie

Georgie Porgie, pudding and pie,
Kissed the girls and made them cry.
When the boys came out to play,
Georgie Porgie ran away.

Mary had a little lamb

Mary had a little lamb
Its fleece was white as snow,
And everywhere that Mary went
The lamb was sure to go.

It followed her to school one day,
Which was against the rule.
It made the children laugh and play
To see a lamb at school.

Baa, baa, black sheep

Baa, baa, black sheep,
Have you any wool?
Yes, sir. Yes, sir.
Three bags full.
One for my master,
And one for my dame,
And one for the little boy
　　who lives down the lane.

Humpty Dumpty

Humpty Dumpty sat on a wall,
Humpty Dumpty had a great fall;
All the King's horses and all the King's men
Couldn't put Humpty together again.

Old King Cole

Old King Cole
Was a merry old soul,
And a merry old soul was he;
He called for his pipe,
And he called for his bowl,
And he called for his fiddlers three.

Every fiddler had a fine fiddle,
And a very fine fiddle had he;
Fee, fiddledee, fiddledee,
Went the fiddlers.
Oh! There's none so rare,
As can compare
With King Cole and his fiddlers three!

Pussy cat, pussy cat

Pussy cat, pussy cat,
Where have you been?
I've been to London to
    look at the Queen.

Pussy cat, pussy cat,
How did you go?
Oh! I just took a motor car
    over the snow.

Pussy cat, pussy cat,
What did you there?
Oh! I frightened a little mouse
    under her chair.

Pussy cat, pussy cat,
Did she ask you to dine?
Yes, on rat pies, boiled mice,
    and gooseberry wine.

The lion and the unicorn

The lion and the unicorn
Were fighting for the crown;
The lion beat the unicorn
All around the town.

Some gave them white bread,
And some gave them brown,
Some gave them plum cake
Then drummed them out of town.

The Queen of Hearts

The Queen of Hearts
She made some tarts,
All on a summer's day.

The Knave of Hearts
He stole those tarts,
And took them clean away.

The King of Hearts
Called for the tarts,
And beat the knave full sore.

The Knave of Hearts
Brought back the tarts,
And vowed he'd steal no more.

I had a little nut tree

I had a little nut tree,
Nothing would it bear,
But a silver nutmeg
And a golden pear.
The King of Spain's daughter
Came to visit me,
And all for the sake
Of my little nut tree.
I skipped over water,
I danced over sea,
And all the birds in the air
Couldn't catch me.

Mary, Mary

Mary, Mary, quite contrary,
How does your garden grow?
With silver bells and cockle shells
And pretty maids all in a row.

One, two

One, two	Buckle my shoe.
Three, four	Knock at the door.
Five, six	Pick up sticks.
Seven, eight	Lay them straight.
Nine, ten	A big fat hen.
Eleven, twelve	Dig and delve.
Thirteen, fourteen	Maids a-courting.
Fifteen, sixteen	Maids in the kitchen.
Seventeen, eighteen	Maids a-waiting.
Nineteen, twenty	My plate's empty.

Little Jack Horner

Little Jack Horner
Sat in the corner,
Eating a Christmas pie;
He put in his thumb,
And pulled out a plum,
And said 'What a good boy am I!'

Hot cross buns

Hot cross buns! Hot cross buns!
One a penny,
Two a penny,
Hot cross buns.

If you have no daughters,
Give them to your sons.

One a penny,
Two a penny,
Hot cross buns.

Jack Sprat

Jack Sprat could eat no fat,
His wife could eat no lean,
And so between the both of them,
They licked the platter clean.

Jack ate all the lean,
Joan ate all the fat.
The bone they picked it clean,
Then gave it to the cat.

Jack Sprat was wheeling
His wife by the ditch,
The barrow turned over,
And in she did pitch.

Says Jack 'She'll be drowned!'
But Joan did reply,
'I don't think I shall
For the ditch is quite dry.'

Old Mother Hubbard

Old Mother Hubbard
Went to the cupboard
To get her poor dog a bone,
But when she got there
The cupboard was bare
And so the poor dog had
  none.

She went to the baker's
To buy him some bread,
But when she came back
The poor dog was dead.

She went to the joiner's
To buy him a coffin,
But when she came back
The poor dog was laughing.

She went to the fish-man's
To buy him some fish,
But when she came back
He was licking the dish.

She went to the barber's
To buy him a wig,
But when she came back
He was dancing a jig.

She went to the tailor's
To buy him a coat,
But when she came back
He was riding a goat.

She went to the cobbler's
To buy him some shoes,
But when she came back
He was reading the news.

The dame made a curtsey,
The dog made a bow;
The dame said 'Your servant.'
The dog said 'Bow wow.'

Three blind mice

Three blind mice! Three blind mice!
See how they run! See how they run!
They all ran after the farmer's wife,
She cut off their tails with a carving knife,
Did you ever see such a sight in your life
As three blind mice?

Simple Simon

Simple Simon met a pieman,
Going to the fair;
Says Simple Simon to the pieman,
'Let me taste your ware?'

Says the pieman to Simple Simon,
'Show me first your penny.'
Says Simple Simon to the pieman,
'Indeed, I have not any.'

Curly Locks, Curly Locks

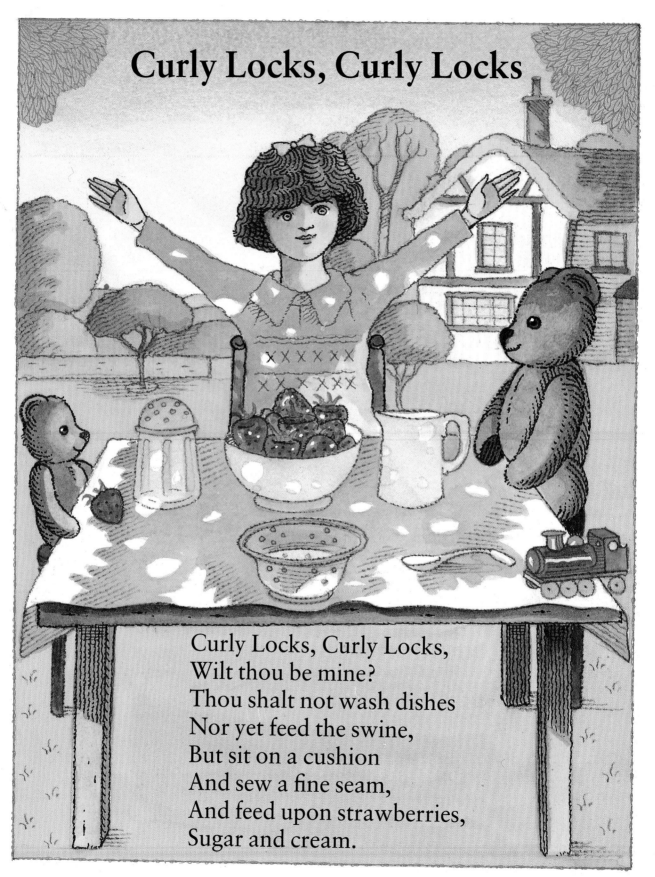

Curly Locks, Curly Locks,
Wilt thou be mine?
Thou shalt not wash dishes
Nor yet feed the swine,
But sit on a cushion
And sew a fine seam,
And feed upon strawberries,
Sugar and cream.

One, two, three, four, five

One, two, three, four, five;
Once I caught a fish alive.
Six, seven, eight, nine, ten;
But I let it go again.

Why did you let it go?
Because it bit my finger so.
Which finger did it bite?
This little finger on my right.

Ding, dong, bell

Ding, dong, bell,
Pussy's in the well.
Who put her in?
Little Tommy Thin.
Who pulled her out?
Little Johnny Stout.
What a naughty boy was that
To try to drown poor pussy cat,
Who ne'er did any harm
But caught all the mice in his father's barn.

Jack and Jill

Jack and Jill went up the hill,
To fetch a pail of water;
Jack fell down
   and broke his crown
And Jill came tumbling after.

Then up Jack got, and home did trot,
As fast as he could caper;
He went to bed to mend his head
With vinegar and brown paper.

When Jill came in, how she did grin
To see Jack's paper plaster;
Her mother, vexed, did whip her next,
For laughing at Jack's disaster.

Little Bo-Peep

Little Bo-Peep has lost her sheep,
And doesn't know where to find them;
Leave them alone, and they'll come home,
Bringing their tails behind them.

Little Boy Blue

Little Boy Blue, come blow your horn,
The sheep's in the meadow,
The cow's in the corn.
Where is the boy
 who looks after the sheep?

He's under a haystack,
Fast asleep.
Will you wake him?
No, not I,
For if I do, he's sure to cry.

Tom, Tom, the piper's son

Tom, Tom, the piper's son,
Stole a pig and away he run,
The pig was eat and Tom was beat,
And Tom went crying down the street.

Tom, Tom, the piper's son,
He learned to play when he was young;
But all the tune that he could play
Was 'Over the hills and far away.'

There was a crooked man

There was a crooked man,
And he walked a crooked mile;
He found a crooked sixpence
Against a crooked stile;
He bought a crooked cat,
Who caught a crooked mouse,
And they all lived together
In a little crooked house.

There was an old woman

There was an old woman
Who lived in a shoe.
She had so many children,
She didn't know what to do.
She gave them some broth
Without any bread,
And whipped them all soundly
Then sent them to bed.

As I was going to St Ives

As I was going to St Ives,
I met a man with seven wives;
Each wife had seven sacks,
Each sack had seven cats,
Each cat had seven kits:
Kits, cats, sacks and wives,
How many were there going to St Ives?

Ladybird, ladybird

Ladybird, ladybird,
Fly away home,
Your house is on fire,
Your children will burn,
All except one,
Her name is Ann,
She crept under the frying-pan.

The north wind doth blow

The north wind doth blow,
And we shall have snow,
And what will poor robin do then?
Poor thing!

He'll sit in a barn,
And keep himself warm,
And hide his head under his wing,
Poor thing!

Little Polly Flinders

Little Polly Flinders
Sat among the cinders,
Warming her pretty little toes.
Her mother came and caught her
And whipped her little daughter
For spoiling her nice new clothes.

I love little pussy

I love little pussy,
Her coat is so warm,
And if I don't hurt her
She'll do me no harm.

So I'll not pull her tail
Nor drive her away,
But pussy and I
Very gently will play.

She shall sit by my side
And I'll give her some food,
And pussy will love me
Because I am good.

Little Tommy Tucker

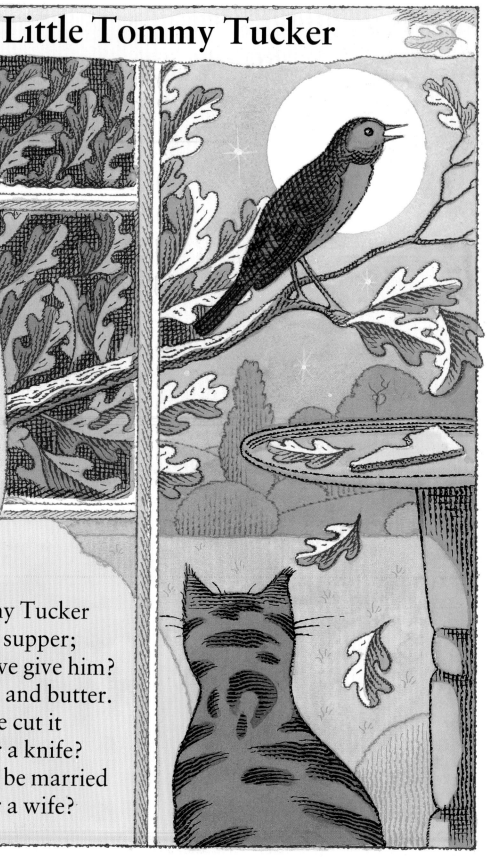

Little Tommy Tucker
Sings for his supper;
What shall we give him?
White bread and butter.
How shall he cut it
Without e'er a knife?
How will he be married
Without e'er a wife?

Goosey, goosey, gander

Goosey, goosey, gander,
Whither shall I wander?
Upstairs and downstairs,
And in my lady's chamber.

There I met an old man
Who wouldn't say his prayers;
I took him by his left leg,
And threw him down the stairs.

Wee Willie Winkie

Wee Willie Winkie,
Runs through the town,
Upstairs and downstairs,
In his nightgown.
Rapping at the window,
Crying through the lock,
Are the children in their beds
For it's now eight o'clock?

Hey! Willie Winkie,
Are you coming then?
The cat's singing pussie,
To the sleeping hen;
The dog's lying on the floor
And does not even peep;
But here's a wakeful laddie,
That will not fall asleep.

Wearied is the mother
That has a restless wean,
A wee, stumpy bairnie
Heard whene'er he's seen;
That has a battle aye with sleep
Before he'll close an e'e,
But a kiss from off his rosy lips
Gives strength anew to me.

The man in the moon

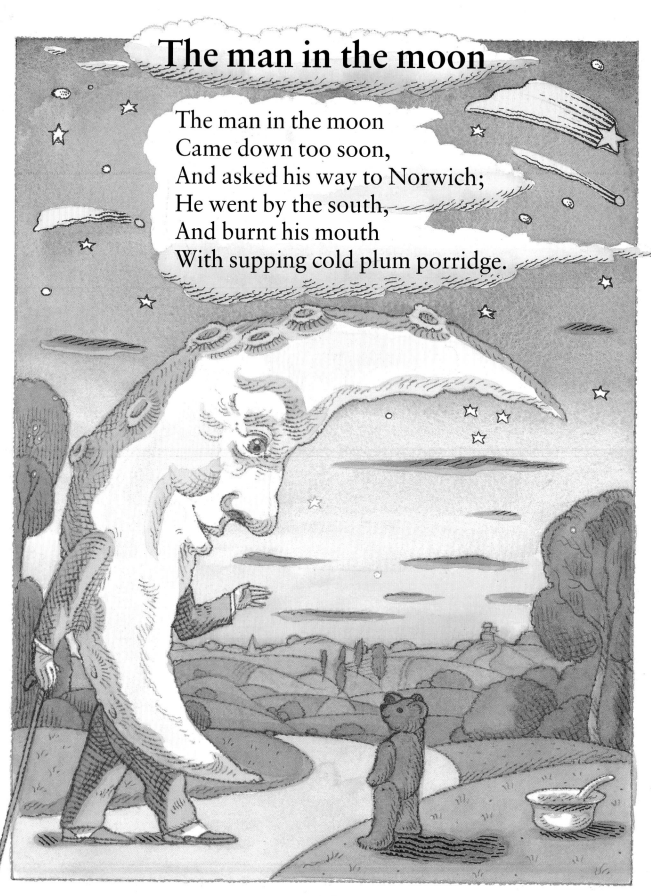

The man in the moon
Came down too soon,
And asked his way to Norwich;
He went by the south,
And burnt his mouth
With supping cold plum porridge.

Hey, diddle, diddle

Hey, diddle, diddle,
The cat and the fiddle,
The cow jumped over the moon.
The little dog laughed
To see such sport,
And the dish ran away with the spoon.

How many miles to Babylon?

'How many miles to Babylon?'
'Three-score miles and ten.'
'Can I get there by candle-light?'
'Yes, and back again,
If your heels are nimble and light,
You may get there by candle-light.'